Dedication

In memory of Empress Ziva, and with heartfelt gratitude
to RSPCA Leeds who brought us together.

Sian Nicholas

The Miaows of Chaircat McGee

AUSTIN MACAULEY PUBLISHERS™

LONDON • CAMBRIDGE • NEW YORK • SHARJAH

A CIP catalogue record for this title is available from the British
Library.

ISBN 9781786934727 (Paperback)
ISBN 9781786934734 (E-Book)
www.austinmacauley.com

First Published (2017)
Austin Macauley Publishers Ltd.
25 Canada Square
Canary Wharf
London
E14 5LQ

Contents

Introduction

I believe strongly that cat-kind has been dumbed-down over recent generations. The cat which has been revered in history as a creature to be worshipped has become seen as nothing more than a plaything, a furry additional extra around the house. The years of wisdom and cat evolution have been negated as cats have become disposable objects.

I say this from bitter experience as my two cat comrades and I are all either rescued or abandoned by our owners. Empress Ziva and I were taken in by the RSPCA after I was found wandering, starving, emaciated and alone living in a wood, and Ziva who was rescued with her two kittens after those renting the house moved out and left her there alone. Dinozzo didn't make it as far as the RSPCA but was rescued by our new carers off the street when it became clear he had been abandoned and was in need of veterinary attention.

In the pages that follow, I hope to redress that balance, and for my readers to understand the right place that all cats should have in any household: at the top of the pecking order. I proffer wit, simple insights in life, love, and loss, and I hope to demonstrate to you the true nature of cathood. I introduce a few new words into the English language such as cattitude and cloggers, share my thoughts on some common human practises, but mostly guide the reader into fully appreciating their role in supporting the cat in their lives. As they say, 'behind every great cat is a minion'.

Right Relationships

The Chinese have a firm cultural principle of harmony within society. Harmony is based upon right relationships, deferring to those in authority over you and of course receiving due deference from those beneath you. This philosophy of right relationships is important to establish for any household where a cat is present. It is essential that all in the household understand who is above them in social rank and status and pay regard to the rules and norms of social behaviour as a result. For harmony to prevail in any catty household, a clear and undisputed pecking order must be established.

This order appears to be in dispute in the household in which I currently reside. The man and woman who live here refer to themselves as 'dad' and 'mum' respectively and expect the level of affection, responsibility and respect that such titles would normally convey. However, even with my elementary grasp of genetics, I am aware that even if the woman and I do share the same colour hair that is genetically really all we have in common. We are not actually related, and I find this felinemorphism of the humans tiring and irritating. They cannot relate to me in my cathood. They will never be my match. Consequently, I like to refer to them as Minion 1 and Minion 2. Minion 1 has the more comfortable lap, is most likely to crumble when asked for food before the allocated time, and the one most willing to give over her space in the bed to me at night. Minion 2 is most likely to poke me awake when I'm sleeping with the words 'sorry, did I wake you', and stuff me in his jacket. You can see which of the two has the greater understanding of true harmony within this household.

The other two occupants of this household, Abi the dog and Dinozzo the other cat, are well aware of their place in regard to right relationship. Abi remains stoically at the bottom of the pecking order, moving herself from the settee, bed, or other item of furniture she is inhabiting so that I can rest my weary bones in the pre-warmed spot. Dinozzo, is the young upstart pretender who has taken over catty leadership since the untimely and unfortunate demise of our true leader Empress Ziva. However, he runs a slack ship, and allows me to steal his food in deference to my greater age, maturity, and appetite.

I feel it is my duty to help all households to develop harmony through the establishment of right relationships, and for cat-kind to take its rightful place at the top of the social ladder.

Communication

It has long been established that cats 'miaow'. However, I think it is fair to say that the range and diversity of cat communication far outstretches this simplistic notion of a two-syllable expression. It is fair to say that Ziva's sole method of communication was a simple 'ow', as she felt no need to tire herself with the first syllable and seemed to be able to convey all her needs with that one noise. Dinozzo too feels that 'less is more' and concentrates on getting his catty needs met through the use of the slightly squeakier 'eek'. True this can sometimes be mistaken for the noise a mouse makes, yet it is compelling, penetrating and effective when combined with the silent 'Doctor Who baddie' type stare.

I, on the other hand, prefer to share a much greater range of noises with my minions. At first, I merely utilised the first syllable that Ziva had declined to use, so that my 'Mah' complemented her 'ow' sublimely. However, I felt this did not convey the full depth of meaning to those beneath me and so have established a fuller complement of vocalisations. I like to employ them whenever I walk because I have a knee that dislocates itself at the drop of a hat: I walk very slowly, and so this naturally extends the length and duration of my various callings. I find this helps in communication.

My favourite speaking voice is the one I use when I want something. This can be food at any time of the day or night, use of the portable lap, stroking, or wiping my nose on the back of Minion 1's hand. It starts with a gentle 'ma' but builds in intensity and pitch until it resembles the sound of a wailing child. I find that this repeated over a period in increasing frequency and pitch will usually precipitate the delivery of my demands.

The communication that I'm most proud of, and use quite frequently at all times of the day and night, is the one I use when I want to trumpet my arrival. This can be inside or out, and is designed to ensure that all in my household, and if outside all the surrounding households, are aware of my presence and are thus duly respectful at my approach. I am assured that this tendency of mine to announce the glad tidings of my arrival contributes in part to our move to a location with fewer neighbours.

Finally, when true harmony has been achieved in the house, and I feel that I have received all the deference I am due, and I have of course given my minions all the affection and attention to which they are entitled I will pronounce harmony with my 'yin yang' expression. I will repeat it several times as I wander around to demonstrate that balance has been achieved in the universe.

The minions babble on regularly and I find the meanings of their words unhelpful and irrelevant. 'Biskies', 'Cat-nap night cap' and 'are you hungry' are the only words a cat truly needs to understand.

Superpowers

There seems to be an obsession with superheroes and villains amongst the human community. My own minions seem to enjoy watching various films and series that involve people being able to do what any self-respecting animal is usually able to do without thinking about it too much. A lot has also been made of animal superpowers in the media recently, and I have watched several documentaries on the topic. However, I feel that these documentaries miss the point. They merely highlight what cats and other animals were meant to do to enable them to live and survive in the world. I feel that humans completely miss out on the real superpowers that animals have.

Take me for example. Due to the fact that I have Feline Leukaemia Virus I have a fairly permanent head-cold. As a result this means that I can cover most things, within a range of about 5 metres, with cat snot at one single sneeze. When feeling particularly affectionate I demonstrate at close range to Minion 1 so that she can feel the full force of my projectile mucus. I can even do this on demand. At a recent trip to the vets my minions and the vet were discussing the colour of my snot at length. In order to assist I produced a large quantity on the examination table for closer inspection.

In addition to my projectile sneezing I can also shed my fur in a projectile manner. This enables Minion 1 to have a much more compact area to hoover as I disperse large clumps of fur over the red carpet on the hall stairs and landing. What is super about this power is that daily I produce enough fur to be able to knit a whole other cat. The rate of my fur growth is phenomenal and would put Rapunzel in the shade. I have been helping the other animals in the household to develop this particular skill as well.

The most useful super power that I have is the ability to tell from 300m and whilst still asleep when my minions decide to have a little nap. I am then able to locate them and remind them of their duties to feed me, and provide a lap/chest/face for me to snooze on with them while they slumber. I am then able to wake them up precisely before they need to be awoken, so that they do not oversleep.

My most awesome superpower must be that of persistence. With it I can open closed bedroom doors, pouches of food, receive physical affection and ensure that Minion 1 turns to the desired position so that I can place myself on the portable lap. I treasure this power the most.

Perversely they do not seem to have the same ability to understand when I need to be woken up, and will on occasions prod me awake with the words 'sorry McGee did we disturb you'. I feel that they are not entirely genuine with their concerns. I cannot for the life of me understand why.

Inter-Species Relationships

I recall with absolute horror the day my minions appeared with Abi. She too was a rescue from the RSPCA; she had been abandoned as a puppy with her litter-mates outside the Bradford RSPCA just after the Christmas holidays and she needed a home. My minions had decided to bring her into our household. I would add with no consultation with either Empress Ziva or myself beforehand. Ziva immediately fluffed up in fully catty fashion and hissed at this 6 month old puppy that had just walked through the door, and I beat a dignified retreat up the stairs where I could view events from a comfortable distance.

The problem with dogs is that they don't understand cats, they don't appreciate our customs or traditions, and they don't try to fit in. They keep on behaving like dogs. There were of course fraught moments as she tried to be friends with us, and we reminded her categorically of where she fitted in the pecking order, and exactly whose house this was. Certainly on at least two or three occasions Ziva had to remind Abi that over-friendliness and a desire to play did not make one a cat, and did not mean that she could chase us across the garden for fun.

However, after a few months we did learn to communicate with each other a little. Both Ziva and I found different ways of engaging this dog in play which was appropriate for us both. Ziva would allow Abi to chase her up the stairs or around the garden, but would tell her immediately when it was time to stop. I for my part, who am less well able to chase around, exhibited my historic and noble relationship to the big cats by crouching down and pouncing on her, so that she ran around the garden in huge loops, occasionally running past me so that I could pounce towards her again and send her off running in loops once more.

There are of course still tensions about who gets what cushion to sleep on, and who has right of residence on the minions' bed during the day. However, mostly we rub along together pretty well. Abi even helped us to 'welcome' Dinozzo into the household when he came to join us off the streets, and taught him the ropes. She was in fact a natural peace-keeper and when Ziva and Dinozzo had a difference of opinion, Abi would come and break up the spat, and monitor the situation until peace prevailed once again. She helps us protect the garden from other cats, squirrels, and foxes, Empress Ziva would always use her as a foot-soldier at times of attack, and she has on occasion rescued me from some aggressive magpies.

She may not be the same species as us, she may not be able to communicate with us as well as we would like, and she may not be a cat, nor does she want to be a cat. Yet, we can respect the differences that we bring to the household, and we can enjoy each other's' company. I even rub heads with her when I return from my regular forays to the local vets.

I do not want to be a dog; she does not want to be a cat. We are what we are, and we like each other, I would go so far as to say we need each other. Surely that's not such a bad thing.

The Portable Lap

One of the many services that my minions provide is the use of the portable lap. My preferred lap is the one carried around by Minion 1, and I will ask to sit on this lap when the mood takes me, usually to have a snooze, and usually when she wants to get up and do something else. The occupation of this lap by another object is in fact 'no object' to me, as I insist on pushing my way on past the obstruction and taking my rightful place in its stead. This includes laptops, which of course work well to pre-warm said portable lap, and also phones, drinks, meals, embroidery or the dog.

The portable lap is occasionally refused to me. This is mostly when the portable lap is situated on the toilet, which I don't understand. Surely if I don't mind where it is, she shouldn't. I guess the portable lap is not a portaloo lap.

On such occasions I have to resort to using the lap of Minion 2. He is generally less obliging about making his lap available for my exclusive use, and will often place me within the confines of his jacket, so that I sit ungainly with my four paws sticking out from under his armpit. Nonetheless I do frequently find myself dropping off in this position, and on a winter's evening it is additional central heating for an old cat.

Should neither portable lap be made available to me, then I am able to demonstrate my displeasure by displacing the dog from whichever comfortable perch she has found for herself. Abi will show her annoyance at my request for her to move but always capitulates to the dominant animal in the room and moves from the settee/chair/minions' bed as requested and can be found skulking in some corner near one of the minions looking grumpy. However, we all know that the winner of the grumpy looking stakes in this household is. I haven't been nicknamed grumplestiltskin for nothing you know.

My favourite activity is to position myself on the portable lap when Minion 1 needs to go to the toilet. I find gentle massage with my paws can render maximum discomfort, this is particularly appropriate when Minion 1 is trying to have a snooze. 5 minutes or so of massage will ensure that not only does she have to get up to go to the toilet, she then has no excuse not to give me one of my regular meals.

Moving House

I am told by my minions that moving house is one of the most stressful things that you will need to do. As I have been forcefully moved by my minions twice in the past 18 months I can now echo that statement from a catty perspective as well. I believe it is a highly over-rated past-time and should be banned immediately for the sake of cat-kind.

Firstly, there is the appearance of large interesting packing boxes; they look enticing but I am not allowed to look into them. What sort of fun is that? Secondly, there is the unexpectedly and suddenly being whisked off to a cattery for a few nights, so that we won't be 'stressed'. I can tell you that having to travel in a tiny container only twice my size, and not being allowed the full dignity that I deserve is highly stressful, and I make my feelings known unreservedly throughout the entire journey. Alongside this I endeavour to make my escape by pawing relentlessly at the bars of the container and make my unhappiness fully felt. If all else fails I reserve sneezing in the face of a minion as they seek to placate me as a last resort in order to avail myself of freedom.

On arrival at the cattery I am usually bundled off to a small room with my other cat comrades. When poor Empress Ziva was with us she would spend the entire time with her head buried under her blanket – she had spent a long time at the RSPCA and had been abandoned so this experience was too reminiscent of her traumatic experiences then of caring for herself and her 2 kittens before being placed in a pen at the RSPCA and eventually finding some new minions to care for her. Dinozzo and myself are far more laid back and more able to cope with these upsets, but the cattery minions do not know our foibles, they do not know that I like to be fed on demand at least 6 times a day, and that I need to have my head rubbed regularly.

Thirdly, we are collected from the cattery and taken to a new location where we are released into the house. I and my colleagues march around the property to examine it closely looking for suitable snoozing and napping locations, and potential escape routes out of the house. We are then detained unlawfully against our wills for a period of time, despite wailing regularly and charging the door when it is open to let the dog in and out. How is it Abi, is allowed to go out and we are not? What has she done to deserve such doggy privileges when we are far higher up the pecking order than she? I am so enraged by this injustice that I am minded to write to Catnesty International to gain my catty rights.

Once we are allowed out after what seems an eternity later I march the property boundary to seek any way out. Because of my dislocating back knee I am unable to jump fences and so have to resort to squeezing under doors or fences. My minions follow me round, pick me up and then block up these exits despite my manifest protests to them that this is not acceptable for any cat. My complaints are ignored and I am held prisoner in the back garden once again.

In an effort to wreak vengeance on the minions for this outrageous behaviour I then spend a significant amount of time waking them up consistently at 3 in the morning by sneezing on them while they slumber...and they thought moving house was stressful. I'll show them what stress is really like after 2 weeks of sleep deprivation.

On Death and Dying

When Empress Ziva died, I felt like the bottom had fallen out of my world. We had both arrived together into our minions care from the RSPCA. We had not been friends there, but we had begun to explore our new home in tandem. I can't say she was an easy cat to get on with, she ruled the roost, put down any vague hint of insurrection, refused to share the space in front of the fire with me, and would on occasion push me over for no good reason that I could see. Yet, sometimes she would clean my face for me and curl up with me on the chair. I have to say that these moments of affection did usually end up in me being roundly cuffed when the whimsy took her, but she did show me affection, and on the days when our minions had deserted us we enjoyed each other's company knowing that we were not truly alone.

She did disappear for 3 weeks on one occasion. I know my minions were fraught with worry looking for her but no matter how much they called and searched the area for her they could not find her. She eventually was found in a nearby house that was being renovated, and my minions caught her and returned her to the fold. It was so good to see her then, but once again she re-imposed the catty order in the household with a double karate chop to my nose when I tried to politely tell her that I had begun sleeping in her favourite spot and would like to continue doing so. I continued this catty duty of rebalancing the household by cuffing the dog immediately afterwards.

Ziva believed in living her full 9 lives. Having been abandoned by her previous minions when she had kittens she had certainly used up 1 of her lives. She was then hit by a car on another occasion but escaped with bruising and a bit of a scare. However, when she contracted Feline Immuno-Virus her catty lives ran out, and a secondary liver infection from which she could not recover meant that she passed away when she was only about 6 years old. It was sudden and unexpected. She had been in rude health more or less until then with only a handful of trips to the vets for vaccinations and check-ups following her disappearance. She was put to sleep and the minions came and buried her in the back garden in the spot that caught the last of the sunlight before the sun set. They placed a paving slab across her grave to stop foxes digging it up and I used to lie on the slab in the sunlight.

Both Dinozzo and I missed her. She had been top-cat, she ran the house, she maintained catty order in the household, and now she was gone. I admit I prefer the more laissez-faire approach to management that Dinozzo operates, but I miss her. I miss rounding a corner and finding her on the cushion. I miss her little 'ow' when she wanted some food; I even miss being cuffed by her when I tried to sit too close to her in front of the fire. Even though we've moved now, and so her scent no longer lingers in the carpets I wonder how she would fit into the new house, how she would have ordered things, and what she would make of it all.

Empress Ziva was truly loved and is truly missed. Although I do not think of her everyday as much as I used to, her presence in my life changed me. I can be glad of the time we had together as refugees from the RSPCA, and I know there is a Ziva shaped space in my heart.

Vets

As a cat of maturity and increasing years, I have found it necessary to spend more of my time in conversation with the local vets. This is a combination of a number of factors, but since I've contracted Feline Leukaemia Virus I have had a number of health issues. My self-dislocating knee is a feature that I have self-managed well over the past 5 years of living with these minions, but I have struggled with a variety of infections which persistently refuse to clear up. The first is a persistent gum infection and the second is a permanent 'head-cold'. All of these mean that on a regular basis I need to travel to the local vet to be inspected, pick up some more antibiotics and have blood tests to check out how my kidneys and liver are doing.

My main aim whilst at the vets is to impress upon them the magnificence of the creature that they have before them. I am able to do this by my charm and winning personality. On the occasions when I have had to stay with them during the day I have chatted to them at length and delighted them with my witty repartee and banter. Whenever I am returned to my minions they are told what a wonderful cat I am, how handsome, how delightful and how I must make their lives so much happier. My minions on the other hand complain that my chatting is pleasant enough for half an hour, but when repeated *ad nauseam* throughout the day and night it is a little wearing. I find their remarks cutting and hurtful. These same minions profess not to care about worldly wealth and pleasures, yet complain that their bank balance is slowly being eroded by frequent trips to the vet and perhaps if they didn't have me they could afford to do things such as going out for an evening occasionally.

The vet's surgery is also another place to demonstrate my amenable nature. Having been bitten by another cat one day I had an abscess from when the wound became infected: this was exceptionally painful. The vet on this occasion had to stick a needle into the lump and remove the pus, and then squeeze the very same out of holes in the abscess. She did all of this without me having a sedative or painkilling injection at that point. The vet was amazed at my docile and amenable nature and though I did think about having a little hiss at one point the truth is it was all much more effort than I could muster.

I dislike being placed in the little crates and like to complain loudly about this. However all in all I do see that the veterinary surgeon is a necessary evil. Because of their help I am coping quite well with my bi-monthly doses of antibiotics and anti-inflammatory drugs, I get to demonstrate to a trained professional how lucky my minions are to have me in their presence, and on occasion I am able to perform party tricks such as returning to my crate on command, or sneezing snot out onto the table on demand.

Vets – you can't live with them but you can't live without them.

Technology

What is it about minions? They spend their entire time glued to their computers, laptops, tablets or smart phones. I'm lucky if I get as much as a look in some days when they're 'surfing the net' for something or other. What happened to real life contact with real life creatures such as my good self, who needs to have his head rubbed, his food bowl filled and the back door opened to a world of opportunities on a very regular basis? I can't fathom why they seek an online community when they have a very real furry community here in this very house, with needs, demands, and enough fur to spread round for all.

I wouldn't mind but on occasion I try to help with the technology. When I'm not using the computer to write my blog I offer them assistance such as pushing the keys on the laptop or PC, or I may try to clean the computer by rubbing the screen with my head. I may even try to help by pushing the touch screen on the laptop and tablet to assist with searches on the internet. Periodically I try to put a protective layer of cat mucus on the screen of all of these items by sneezing upon them. If only they realised the protective qualities that cat mucus holds, especially when it is green. They need not worry about a cracked or scratched screen ever again. It is true that they might not be able to see the actual screen through the layers of cat mucus, but I think that's a very small price to pay.

On occasions they put their phones down and cannot remember where they have left them. They then have to get one of their other phones to 'ring' the lost phone in order to locate it. This obviously works unless they have run out of battery power, put the phone on silent, or dropped it down the toilet.

I have a much more effective location device. It works a little like the echo-location devices that bats and dolphins use in that they send out a signal, it bounces off objects and they are able to locate their prey as a result of these signals that they emit. Mine is a similar technique. I yowl as loudly as I can, the noise bounces around the house, and whatever time of day or night if I continue this noise a minion will either shout and tell me where they are located, or come and pick me up and put me on their bed. This is the best sort of echo-location. I can locate my minions in a very short space of time as they come to my location to find me. Who needs fancy technology when a big voice box and an echoey house are all that is needed?

My favourite piece of technology is the cat-flap which only allows Dinozzo and me into the house because it works from our microchips. This means that no other cat can sneak in and nab our food. It allows us access in and out of the house, but keeps us safe from cat-burglars in the night. This is the best sort of technology. I just need something now that will dispense food on command…oh I forgot, I have something already…. my minions.

Sport

As a cat I am used to the concept of Sport – I like to sport with things for fun, such as the dog. I can spend quite some time pushing her around from piece of furniture to furniture just for the sake of it, or because I want my minions to do something for me and they are slow to respond. On occasion I may even engage in more strenuous activities such as causing the dog to run round the garden in big loops as I reprise my role as a 'big cat'. Or, I may choose to sport with my minions by seeing how many times I can wake them up in the night before they throw something at me. The best bit of sport we ever had was when we managed to drag a dead squirrel in through the cat-flap and leave it in the dining-room for the minions to find. They still haven't worked out how we managed that one yet.

However, the minions seem to engage in another activity they call sport. As far as I can tell it involves sitting on the settee in the living room, watching the television and then leaping up and down, shouting and waving their arms in the air. I know not what causes this behaviour, or quite how it relates to 'sport', but they do seem to do a lot of it. I am a placid amenable chair cat and so these things cause me little bother; I don't mind as long as they don't dislodge me from their lap while they are jumping around. Abi on the other hand finds the loud volumes necessary quite unpleasant and sometimes seeks assurance that no-one is angry with her. I don't know why as no-one is ever angry with her.

I understand that one of the causes of this 'sport' at the moment is the rugby world cup. Both minions are keen fans, by which I mean, both minions jump up and down and shout a lot at the television when this game is on. I even overhead Minion 2 saying to Minion 1 the other day, "look what you've done to me, I care whether Japan wins or not". However, the air is always a bit more subdued when England play Wales at this sport. I am not a cat of national allegiance. I appreciate the cultural lessons to be learned from a variety of nations such as China, Afghanistan, Uganda or Bradford; however I do not get excited by jingoistic sentiment or fervour. However, in the matter of rugby the minions are divided in their loyalties. Minion 1 supports Wales and Minion 2 supports England, so during these games the air can be quite tense and one of the minions is always unhappy at the result.

There is less disagreement on other sports, or other matches, but still I find it all a little unnecessary. Surely no more activity is needed than that which is appropriate to get a cat from the bed to the food bowl to the back garden where they can lie in the sun for a couple of hours before returning to the food bowl and so to bed. Why do minions put their hopes on the joys and successes of a team of people who they've never met, when they could model their lives on the minimal output and quiet self-restraint of a cat? I will never be worried about tyre degradation; I will never worry about the off-side rule. I will never worry about why the England cricket team appear to score more runs in a one day match than in the whole five days of a test match.

Eat, sleep, eat and sleep, and wind up the dog, what else can any cat want in life?

Gardening

I am a cat of the great outdoors. Before finding my way to the RSPCA I spent some time living in the woods by myself, where I learned to appreciate the value of a thick coat and a tree to shelter under, as well as the kindness of strangers who fed me. Since that time I have regularly enjoyed the pleasure of a morning, afternoon or evening in the garden in the sunshine, or on occasion sitting under a tree while the rain falls around me. There is something bracing about the fresh air, the birds flitting around, and the potential possibility of escape.

However, the minions seem to find it impossible to sit in the garden for any length of time to enjoy the sheer pleasure of sitting and being. They are always doing something which usually involves noisy, smelly, or sharp bits of machinery. Minion 2 is always mowing the lawn and complaining about the bits of stick that the dog leaves in the grass for him to pick up. Since we have moved, Minion 1 can be found in the garden on a daily basis with her trusty lopper, bow saw and secateurs cutting back the green jungle that threatens to over-run the space that we have. She spends several hours a day removing branches and even whole trees and has learned to deftly use a pickaxe and mattock in her attempts to dig out the roots of these plants. On one such root removal Minion 1 found a whole area of path that had been buried beneath undergrowth and possibly had not been seen for over a decade. They have renamed the garden 'the lost civilisation of Sutton Coldfield' for this reason.

The dog benefits from all of this undergrowth clearing by the appearance of a range of balls that have been left by the former doggy inhabitants of the house. The benefits to a cat of these clearing activities are the sudden appearance of large areas of soft, very diggable, soil. In order to make a contribution to these herculean digging efforts Dinozzo and I like to contribute our very own specialised form of fertilizer which is high in nitrogen and other amino acids and can be dug into the soil with minimal effort. For some reason these efforts are not appreciated and our attempts at 'helping' are frowned upon. Therefore our days are spent finding comfortable resting places upon the wormery, or a tarpaulin, or currently upon the carpet which has been placed to kill off the grass on the site of the chicken coop.

We are hopeful that eventually we will have shrubs and flowers blossoming in the garden rather than a sea of holly and ivy and laurel bushes, and that we can gambol happily amongst the plants trying to swat butterflies and being told off for trying to catch the bees. My minions report that this is likely to be several months away.

As I am now in my dotage, I look forward to these halcyon days of leisure and rest, and I think the minions are hopeful that when this day comes for me they too will be able to sit in the garden and enjoy watching the birds, the squirrels, the butterflies and the bees as well. I shall continue to help by keeping up the guerrilla fertiliser activities when they're not looking. These minions, they just don't know how lucky they are.

Sleep

Being crepuscular predators active mostly at dawn and dusk, cats have a great deal of spare time to accommodate. We are able to do this most spectacularly through our ability to sleep for many hours at a time, usually up to and including 20 hours of sleep in any 24 hour period. As you can imagine, we have honed this task down to a fine art and are able to continue sleeping at a moment's notice having been disturbed, or having woken up for food. Cats are also able to sleep in the strangest of places, yet I find that as in many things the secret to a good snooze is location, location, location.

Generally I seek the softest and warmest place available. On a sunny day I am prepared to sacrifice softness for a spot in the sun instead though if the two can be combined, such as when the sun hits the minion's bed, then this is of course most desirable. Additionally I find that I like to generally have my head resting gently on some part of Minion 1's anatomy. At night I like to lie with my head on the back of her hand. This serves two purposes, it enables me to gently wipe cat mucus from my nostrils onto the back of her hand and so aid breathing whilst asleep and secondly it means that when she stops stroking my chin and chest with her fingers I can dig my one remaining canine into the back of her hand to get her to restart until I fall asleep.

From first glance one would believe that cats do very little whilst they sleep, but let me assure you we are masters of multi-tasking at this time. I personally have run several laps of an Olympic stadium whilst asleep as I have chased squirrels, mice and the dog during moments of REM sleep. Additionally I am able to engage in shedding fur and with that dirt that has got caught up in it leaving a small ginger indentation wherever I lay. I understand that it is for this reason that the minions have started to use multi-coloured patterned duvet covers so that the fur and dirt doesn't show up so much. Furthermore, though asleep I am able to tell when the minions have settled down to watch TV so that I can then join them on the comfort of the settee and continue to rest my head on minion 1's hand to help with mucus drainage.

They say that cats sleep lightly, and it is true that on occasion I am disturbed by the slightest noise. However as I grow older, baggier and saggier at the seams quite often my minion will need to give me a good shake to wake me up for my nightly metacam. As king of the jungle I have delegated responsibility for my protection to the dog, and so it is her duty to ensure that my life is not under threat of harm, which enables me to fall into such deep slumberous moments. When my minions fall into such moments though I feel it is my duty to ensure their protection by awaking them and alerting them to any potential threats. As I am quite deaf and often don't hear these potential threats I feel it is better to be safe than sorry and so wake them up periodically through the night just to be on the safe side. I'm sure they'll thank me for it one day.

Bees

There seems to be quite a furore in the media these days about bees. Honeybees or bumblebees, they are all considered to be very important. My minions have placed a moratorium upon hunting, swatting, pouncing and generally attempting to kill such creatures stating that they are 'our friends'. To this end we have two beehives in the garden from which these little winged creatures flit backwards and forward depending upon the ambient temperature.

I have to say that although taken as individuals I do not mind bees, and may while away a happy few moments watching them buzz around a flower or shrub, en masse they are quite something different. On warm days the air is often very busy with them as they flit to and from their hives. To be fair they tend to ignore me, yet they make quite a noise and in a large group look quite scary.

About once a week the 2 minions get dressed up in some very strange clothing, which means that they have a mesh over their heads and are fully covered, and they take the top off the hives and look inside. I often see them at this time and like to come over to say hello, but I am very unceremoniously shooed away on these occasions, and even once or twice with a gentle shoving of a gum-booted toe. This I feel is well below my station and I do not understand how they can consider the welfare of these horrid little buzzing creatures to be more important than my general needs for affection and food on demand.

I also understand that honeybees are so called because they are supposed to provide the minions with honey. It appears though that despite several seasons of bee owning, and attempting to grow the number of hives in the garden, the bees have consumed more in sugar syrup prepared for them by the minions, than the minions have ever consumed in honey from the bees. Personally, I think this is a good thing because if an animal is kept purely because it is supposed to earn it's keep, then I am in deep trouble, costing on average far more in vets fees and food on a monthly basis than the minions ever claw back from the sale of cat-fur stuffed cushions, or the ginger hair extensions they sell at the local hairdressers. They have considered using me for modelling purposes, but I understand that my craggy good looks and rough exterior are not so much in demand these days from pet-food companies who prefer the prettier, cuter cat.

Nonetheless it appears that the bees are with us to stay. They do provide another dimension to the garden, and it is quite pleasant watching them from a distance as they go about their merry way. I understand that they are at threat from pesticides and pests such as varroa mite. Although I do not know what these things are, or how they impact the bees, I would be very sad to live in a garden without bees, even if they don't produce any honey for the minions. After-all, I am sweet enough for them both.

Pets as Therapy

No one can dispute the therapeutic value of animal ownership: the pleasure of stroking a soft warm furry body is well documented to reduce stress levels in all, and aid recovery for those who are unwell. There are many dedicated volunteers who take their pets into a variety of places to allow strangers to stroke them and to feel the benefit of animal love and affection.

To be a 'Pets as Therapy' animal it needs to be placid and gentle, able to cope with strangers and loud noises and to enjoy meeting new people. Abi, my canine living companion is one such dog, and she has been registered as a 'Pets as Therapy' dog. She has up until now had limited placements but has enjoyed making new friends at church and at coffee mornings, where all have been pleased to see her and to make a fuss of her, in fact more pleased to see her than the minions who take her.

It is well known that Cats too can be 'Pets as Therapy' animals. Although not a registered PAT animal, I believe that Bob the Street Cat, that celebrated feline ginger tom, is an excellent example of the impact that a cat can have upon the life of someone in desperate need of some unconditional love and affection. In addition other cats around the country don a harness or lead and enter the lives of men, women and children to offer them some catty love. Who would not benefit from such rarefied attention? Who could not immediately feel relaxed and calm receiving warmth and love from so noble a creature as a cat?

My minions have considered registering me as a 'Pets as Therapy' cat. I am after all very placid, can fall asleep on a lap at a moment's notice and really do not care whose lap it is as long as it is warm and dry and they have a hand to rub my head with. Visitors to the house have often expressed their amazement at my friendly and talkative nature. Who would not want to listen to the endless advice and counsel such a wise cat as myself could offer regarding the resolution of life's little problems? Who would not feel the stress and worries of life float away as I gently massaged their stomach with my paws as I sought to get a more comfortable resting place.

Unfortunately all 'Pets as Therapy' animals must be fit and well. With my dodgy back leg and my permanent head-cold this rather precludes me from joining the ranks of these worthy animals. Apparently no-one's stress levels are reduced by a cat sneezing in their face at point-blank range or having a little hacking choky fit whilst sitting on their lap, and amusing as it is, no-one feels relaxed watching a cat lose its balance when either of these 2 things happen. Apparently these things are not therapeutic. I for the life of me cannot understand why. Does no-one understand the healing properties of cat snot? Rubbed into someone's chest it provides a good embrocation for all sorts of ills.

However, it seems that 'darling Abi' remains the socially acceptable creature who is allowed to shed her doggy charm and healing powers on all who come near, whereas I just get to shed fur and mucus. Oh well, that's better than nothing I suppose, and I shall continue to provide all visitors to the house with this delightful service whether they like it or not.

Loyalty

I understand in common cultural parlance loyalty is not a trait that is often attributed to cats: It is our counterparts who are given all the credit for loyalty. Statues are built to dogs such as Gelert who saved his master's son from the wolves and was killed by his master by mistake. Or Greyfriars Bobby, the Skye terrier who reputedly spent 14 years refusing to leave his owner's grave until he himself died. Dogs are often valorised by people as being loyal. Loyalty itself is a prised commodity amongst humans; people expect loyalty from their partners, their children, their friends and their employees. I have no qualms with desire for loyalty, but I believe that people are often wrong in considering some actions to be more demonstrative of loyalty than others.

As I said before, dogs are considered to be loyal and cats are considered to be fickle creatures by their minions. However, I do beg to differ. Who is it that sits outside keeping Minion 1 company whilst she works in the garden in all weathers? It is I and quite often Dinozzo will join in for a while if he doesn't have a more important place to snooze. It is I that sits quietly under the tree while my fur gets gently damper in the rain and the dog waves her paw nonchalantly from the warmth of the living-room as she watches through the patio doors. It is I that exercises the dog by chasing her around the garden when she would like a second walk and Minion 1 is too busy to take her. It is I that does not claw my minions to death when they force feed me four antibiotics a day for 10 days – surely a fate that they deserve. It is I that keeps them warm at night with my little furry body in the depths of winter, and I who wakes them up in the middle of the night when there are any scary noises outside.

It is I who continues to greet them when they have abandoned me to go on holidays and have left some other minion to care for me – I remain loyal to them even though they have deserted me in the comfort of their home and the care of a capable minion. It is I who gently covers their furniture with cat fur and cat snot to help protect it from the elements. It is I who seek their laps to comfort them when, if truth be told, I'd much rather sleep on the comfort of their bed. It is I who breaks their way into the bedroom at night when they have locked me out to demonstrate my undying love and affection for them.

Ultimately it is I, Chaircat McGee, who demonstrates the epitome of loyalty to my minions. Do they recognise this, do they appreciate it: not in the slightest. I shall however, continue to exhibit these signs of loyalty and caring for my minions. It is right as the more senior creature to care for them and show loyalty, much as I expect them to show me the same unswerving loyalty, support and care as I reach my dotage. Let us only hope they are up to the task.

Squirrels

Our new home is blessed with a number of oak trees in its environs. At the front we have a huge oak tree which must be many years old and happily spreads its boughs to within touching distance of the house. At the back over the fence we have about 30 very tall and leggy oaks that are trying to slowly encroach on the back garden. The immediate offshoot of this is that all creatures that like to eat acorns have taken up permanent residence in the garden. Just yesterday I counted 6 woodpigeons in the front garden with 5 squirrels all digging round amongst the fallen leaves. It drives the dog apoplectic as she seeks to chase them away but is denied by the minions.

The squirrels are a mixed blessing in many ways. They do provide plenty of entertainment as they scurry around the gardens, either playing/fighting with each other or trying to escape from Abi who has been sat for 10 minutes silently at the top end of the garden waiting for one of them to appear. They do also seem to spend a lot of time burying acorns as well; in the lawn, in the borders, in the leaf litter, under trees, in plant-pots, in fact anywhere there is a surface which is soft enough in which to bury a nut. I am no expert, and as an older feline I have to admit my memory is not what it was, but I am confident that they cannot possibly remember all these locations.

Like hammy from 'over the hedge' surely they must on occasion 'lose their nuts'.

Also, Dinozzo finds the whole scenario of being top predator far too wearing with this many squirrels to chase, and after giving chase to one or two will sit resignedly staring intently at some small creature in the ivy with his back to the squirrels that are cavorting on the lawn behind him. I think he believes that if he isn't looking at him then they can't see him. This of course, would be anathema to Empress Ziva who in her life with us caught and slew at least 2 squirrels, one of which she cat-handled through the cat-flap and left as an offering to our minions in the dining-room. They of course did not appreciate either act of bravery and both presents were unceremoniously dropped in the bin.

However recently, I have joined forces with Dinozzo, and despite being older and not so nimble on my feet am able to flush a squirrel toward a tree. If Dinozzo sits quietly behind the tree he is able to surprise the squirrel as it rushes headlong toward its presumed escape, and pounce on it. We successfully achieved this hunting activity just recently, although the squirrel was really only batted by Dinozzo and made good his escape over the back fence. I, of course, went to his escape route and checked that he had indeed gone and stood guard there for some time to ensure he did not return. Dinozzo continued to sit in the exact same position he had pounced on as he re-lived his moment of glory.

I fear we are unlikely to be successful in our bid to catch and kill a squirrel entirely: the bell on Dinozzo's collar remains a liability in our efforts to surprise these creatures. However, we remain hopeful that this

Christmas our minions will have an extra special treat under the tree on Christmas morning.

Foxes

When our minions collected us from the RSPCA, they had to sign a form stating they would not let us out at night. This is partly for two reasons: the first being that cats are more likely to be run over by cars at night, and the second being that foxes are considered to be a threat to cats. Despite being old and somewhat wobbly on my feet I would like to paraphrase that great rabbit General Woundwort from 'Watership Down' when I state categorically – that in my opinion 'foxes are not dangerous'.

Why should I be so bold as to make so wild a claim? From personal experience, I have encountered several foxes in my life. In our first home in Bradford we had two foxes that lived nearby and frequented our garden regularly. During the winter they were often to be seen in daylight hours out and about, often rolling around in our vegetable patch, and so we came across them quite often. When Abi wasn't with us – her presence did rather preclude the foxes staying in the garden – I have observed foxes seeking to play with different cats, they would play-bow, and then run backwards and forwards as the cat pounced upon them, much as Abi does when she wants to play with me. My minions even managed to record it because they could not believe it.

This activity was not restricted to these particular foxes in Bradford either. When we moved we had a family of 3 foxes that lived next door. Again they would regularly appear in our garden in daylight hours. On one such occasion I happened to be taking my rest on the foxy-made path that led to their escape route from the garden. I was tired, as is often the way for an older cat, and so I refused to move. Every time the fox came near me I would miaow at him to show my disgruntlement and refusal to budge. The fox did not seek to get past me, in fact he was quite anxious as he looked round for other escape routes from the garden and eventually disappeared elsewhere. Admittedly I am a big cat for a domestic creature, and am probably not much smaller than the fox, and if I don't move then the fox could not see that I am actually a disabled cat and would not be able to defend myself well in a fight. In this case staying still and miaowing my disapproval was probably the best thing to do. In any event the fox was not a threat to me.

I have also observed the foxes trying to encourage Dinozzo to play. He is a much smaller looking cat, and was still quite kittenish at that point. Although a little uncertain, Dinozzo did engage in playing a little with the fox before it headed off.

I am sure the RSPCA are not wrong, and that foxes can be a threat to cats, but my advice is not to assume the worst, be prepared to defend yourself, but even though they come in wolf's clothing, they can sometimes be more sheep-like than you'd expect.

Trees

Cats are rumoured to love climbing trees and occasionally to get stuck in them. Empress Ziva was always a keen tree climber, though as I recall always managed to navigate her way back down. She did on several occasions get stuck on the roof of the house, but as only a bathroom window needed to be left open to facilitate her escape it was never a particularly traumatic experience for her. Dinozzo too will occasionally fling himself halfway up a tree to get a better view of his environs and has sat in a tree watching aerosol cans and other flammable items exploding from a previous neighbours' bonfire in Bradford.

Personally, climbing trees is not a past-time that I am able to undertake due to my dodgy back leg, but nonetheless I am a keen fan of trees. I enjoy sitting out under their shade both in the heat of the day, and also when it is raining. At times, during particularly heavy downpours, I will wait patiently under a tree while one of the minions dons a coat and comes out to collect me and tuck me under his or her coat to keep me dry to bring me back indoors. However, the new garden where we now live has a surfeit of trees. There are too many, they are too 'leggy' and they cut out the light to the garden which is necessary to enable the nectar-producing plants to grow for our bees and so they are being 'thinned'.

For thinning to take place Minions 1 and 2 have availed themselves of some garden equipment to enable the cutting and removal of tree branches etc. Minion 2 in particular is quite keen on these and has enjoyed defying death by climbing ladders wielding some of the noisier sharper implements. On these occasions I feel it is incumbent upon me to lend a hand to proceedings. I like to draw near and watch from close by, and I feel that the best viewing spot is directly below the branch or tree limb they are at that moment trying to chop off. It gives me a clear line of sight to miaow instructions as they hack away at the relevant piece of wood. For some reason this produces the most odious reactions from Minion 1, who is usually standing at the base of the ladder doing very little from what I can see. She starts shouting at me to go away. Of course I ignore these words: a good supervisor never leaves his workforce on their own when they are clearly in need of instruction. When this happens she becomes even more annoying and will pick up anything she can reach, without letting go of the bottom of the ladder, and throw it at me. Fortunately she is not a very good shot and has yet to actually hit me. However, I can see that my good intentions are not welcomed and with an appropriate air of disdain I will make my way to a new viewing location while the minions continue with their activities.

I do try to contribute in other ways, and have chosen a particular Hawthorn tree in the garden to attack on a regular basis with my claws. I feel that over a significant period of time, by showing this particular tree who is boss and by scratching my claws there when necessary, I can help in my own way to the 'thinning out' of the trees in our garden. We shall see who is most successful the minions or me – I am sure with my superior persistence, catty skills, and in-built toolkit that I will prevail.

Christmas

I have now lived with these particular minions for 5 years. Generally they have served me well, and seem to be reasonably level-headed and trustworthy creatures. It is for this reason that I and Dinozzo have opted to remain with them, despite their obvious failings and tendency to not allow me to sleep on their lap at every available opportunity. However, there seems to be some strange custom that takes place every year during the winter. I believe it is called 'Christmas'.

As Minion 2 is a vicar, this means that he appears to be very busy during this time, running backwards and forwards between the house and the church, whilst Minion 1 appears to spend her time cutting down large sections of garden shrubbery, tying them into some sort of decorative configuration and then leaving them festooned all over the house. I wouldn't mind but it appears they have spent some considerable time in this new house removing excess holly, ivy and fir trees from the garden, and now these unwanted items are appearing inside the house. I mean literally, the fir tree that was standing at 18 foot tall in the front garden is now significantly shorter and inside the living room. What is a cat supposed to make of that? As I mentioned previously, I'm not a great tree climber but in any event we are not allowed to touch the tree, scratch it, or attempt to climb it.

What is the point of that I ask? Why have something from the outside inside and then not be able to treat it as if it was still outside? In addition Minion 1 decorates the house with these little twinkly lights, and places them on the tree. Consequently, this large shrub is covered in electrical items, and has presents placed underneath it, and is then left in the corner of the room like some Martian visitor.

We then have human visitors who come for Christmas. They don't have decorations or lights put on them, but they do hang around in the living room. I like visitors, they tend to stroke me and let me sit on their laps. However, too many visitors mean that there may not be space enough on the settee for me to sleep. It also means that the bedroom doors that were hitherto left open for our personal use of the beds are now closed. We are left to undertaking surreptitious sneak attacks into the bedroom when the inhabitants pop to the toilet in the night so that we can get onto the bed, because obviously the bed in the room with the closed door is far preferable to the bed in the room with the door left deliberately open so we can sleep in there.

I know, because these things have happened in previous years, that suddenly one day, for no reason, shortly after the human visitors have left, this Martian visitor will also suddenly have outstayed its welcome and will be removed. I will walk into the living room one day and there will be no sight or sound of the tree. All the decorations will be gone and life will be restored to normal once again. I don't understand this traditional practice, it seems a strange human custom and I don't see much in it for me. However, as long as I continue to get a catty present each year, I'll allow this yearly disturbance in my catty routine.

Fur

One of the reasons that cats are so loved is due to the copious quantities of fur that they possess. I believe you can find hairless cats, known as Sphynx cats, and I understand that they were bred in the 1960's. Their skin is the colour that their fur would be and they do have a soft downy fur, but in my opinion nothing that a cat could either be truly proud of, or that could serve to keep him sufficiently warm on a cold winter's night. I mean it gets to -25C in Canada some nights during the winter– what are these people thinking?

I however have copious amounts of fur. It is thick and luxurious and I like to share it with my minions on every occasion in every location. I like to leave them large clumps of ginger fur on the carpet, on the wooden stairs, on their clothing, and most definitely on the duvet cover of their bed. I am confident that if they collected it up I could save them a fortune in loft insulation. In addition it means that I can go outside when it is cold, or wet, or sunny and my fur protects me from the extremes of the weather. Even if it is raining, unless it is a deluge, my fur acts to keep me dry. Although I'm not keen on snow my fur keeps me relatively dry and warm. It also enables me to lie very close to any source of heat and to soak up that heat without becoming too hot or burning. In the summer I can lay for ages following the sun around the garden or house and lying in as hot a spot as I can find with no ill effects. Fur is in fact a truly marvellous thing.

Being furry does have a few problems though. In order to keep myself looking beautiful and pristine I must groom myself meticulously. It takes a lot of effort to remain this craggily handsome at my age. However, because I also have more snot than your average cat, and because I suffer with hairballs, the fur/snot combination does have the occasional side-effect whereby it gets lodged in the back of my throat and I have to spend some time hacking away in an effort to remove it. I like to try to keep these times to the wee small hours of the morning when I am asleep on my minions' bed so that they can pat me on the back of the shoulders to help me in dislodging the furry mucusy mass. I am sure they don't mind having their sleep disturbed in the slightest, it is after all their deepest desire to serve me.

Dinozzo is a black cat, whose fur is less thick though equally prone to being shared with the minions. This morning my minion showed me a photo of a cat which appeared to be half-ginger tom and half black[1]. It looked as if Dinozzo and I had 'morphed' into one cat. I'm not sure what personality a Dinozzo/McGee combination of cat would have, but it surely couldn't be as good as 100% McGee.

My minions like my fur, in fact Minion 2 often suggests that when I am no more that they will skin me and use me as a hearthrug. All I can say is 'over my dead body'.

---

[1] Venus the Two-Faced Cat
https://twitter.com/Venustwofacecat

New Year Resolutions

There appears to be a tradition amongst human minions to make a 'resolution' at the beginning of the year because they feel that there is something that needs to be changed in their lives and they want to make this change for the better. I take issue with this practice for a number of reasons. The first being 'New Year': it is an entirely arbitrary time of year. There are different New Year's celebrated throughout the Gregorian calendar, only one of which starts on January the 1st.

The Chinese have a New Year in February; this year it's February the 8th because it's on a lunar calendar and so changes every year. They have a different animal for each year which in 2016 it is the year of the Monkey. The only resolution that a monkey would need to make is to be more like a cat, surely. Across the Indian Sub-Continent and through Afghanistan, Iran and other countries the New Year is celebrated on March the 21st, recognised as the first day of spring, which in my mind makes more sense than the 1st of January. Surely spring is when new life and the New Year truly begin: though with climate change who knows when spring will begin in future years.

There are of course religious New Years as well. The 5th Sunday before Christmas is the beginning of advent and the Christian New Year, and the Jewish New Year is

Rosh Hashanah and starts on the 2nd of October. Equally, the Muslim New Year is also in October but on the 3rd. These are both on a lunar cycle. Other religions and other New Years are available. So you can see, New Year is a truly arbitrary concept, and thus making resolutions to change based on the arrival at a completely random moment in time seems fairly ridiculous to a wise old sage such as myself.

However, if I were to impart some wisdom on the subject of resolutions I would say the following. Make your resolution quite specific, not 'to be a better cat' but how would you be a better cat (if such a thing were possible). I, for example, might resolve not to push the dog off her spot on the bed/settee/chair/rug just because I can. I won't resolve to do this, of course, but you get the idea. The resolution should also be something that you know how many times you have done it. So, I might resolve to wake my minions up only once during the night instead of 3 times and thus, I know if I have succeeded in doing this or not. Thirdly, the resolution needs to be something that is actually possible. I might resolve to climb to the top of the oak tree outside our front door for exercise each day, but I know that with my gammy leg I am unable to do so. Instead I can resolve to get Dinozzo to do this for me because he's much younger and fitter than I am. Fourthly, do I have time and energy to undertake this resolution? If I state that each day I will guard the garden from squirrels for at least 2 hours, then where and when am I going to get all my sleeping in? Let's be realistic here: what are the other commitments that I have which I need to meet that are more important or immovable.

Finally, how long am I going to give myself to change: they say it takes 3 months to make a habit and so perhaps if I made a resolution I would review it after 3 months to see if I had been successful, if I needed more resolve or if I needed to tweak it a little. As for personal resolutions, I won't be making any. I am of course a perfect cat, who needs to change nothing about myself, though I have a long list of suggested resolutions for my minions beginning with: 'to revere McGee with greater adoration by feeding him fresh chicken daily'....

Illness

As a cat of indeterminate but mature years I have had my fair share of experience with ill-health. When I was first rescued by the RSPCA I had been woefully neglected and was very underweight – something that I have generally sought to ensure has not been repeated – and quite poorly. Since this time it has transpired that I have been infected with Feline Leukaemia Virus, have a heart murmur (grade II – though not like a listed building), and have a self-dislocating knee joint. My FeLV means that I have a permanent head cold and inflammation of the gums which has led to the removal of most of my teeth so that I now only have about 3 teeth in my head and generally survive by sucking the jelly and gravy off the meat that I'm given. I am, however, a stoic amongst cats. These different maladies have crept upon me slowly over the years and I have got used to them, and I have at least stopped getting the regular bouts of cystitis which affected my little tinky-winky so badly when I needed to pee. That is very inelegant and undignified for a cat of my stature.

A necessary but irritating feature of being ill is the regular trips to the vet and the medication that I need to take as a result. I have written about the vets on previous occasions and generally I don't mind being examined as I like to show off my various skills, abilities and downright charm to as many people as possible. My issue is with the medication that I have to take on a daily basis. For the congestion in my nose I have a de-congestant which is sprinkled on my food twice a day, and in addition the vet has just suggested a second de-congestant for when I'm really bunged up and snotty. All this is on top of the home-made steam baths that Minion 1 makes up with Vicks vaporub in them, or the times that I wake up to find a vaporub soaked tissue placed under my nose whilst I've been sleeping.

Secondly I have to take antibiotics on a bi-monthly basis at the moment. Imagine the indignity of being tucked under Minion 1's arm and having a tablet placed at the back of my throat and then having my mouth held shut so I can't spit it out. This often happens twice in the morning and twice in the evening. I mean what is up with them!? I've recently been given a new type of medication which is squirted into my mouth – it's supposed to be palatable, but all I can say is that whoever made it doesn't have quite the discerning palate that I have. This antibiotic was changed from the one originally prescribed because the first kind was so bad it made me throw up, and I had to waft my tail quite vigorously to demonstrate my disapproval to Minion 1.

Finally, I have to take an anti-inflammatory to help with my knee, the inflammation in my gums and the inflammation in my sinus'. It's just the one dose of medicine but I can tell you during the day I'm up and down like the Assyrian empire with all the medication I have to take.

Far be it from me to complain. I know the minions are only doing their best, and I do feel better as a result of all the medicine, but I do dream of the days when I could run, jump, eat and breathe freely when I was a young cat. I mean I do literally dream of those days and as I lay on the bed or settee I undertake a whole gymnastic routine as I run and jump pain-free chasing rats and mice and squirrels to my little murmuring hearts content. My minions tell me that they are grateful that I am generally quite co-operative with my medicine consumption and it is completed without scratching or hissing. I tell them 'why do you think I keep on waking you up in the middle of the night? I have to get my revenge somehow and there's only so much you can do with 3 teeth'.

Inscrutability

[in-skroo-tuh-buh l]:

1. incapable of being investigated, analysed, or scrutinized; impenetrable.

2. not easily understood; mysterious; unfathomable: an inscrutable smile.

Related forms: Inscrutability (noun)[2]

The characteristic of being inscrutable or our inscrutability is a feature which I believe endears us to our human minions. They who wear their hearts on their sleeve, who seek to share their thoughts and emotions at the drop of a hat on social media, and seek to be known and understood are overwhelmed by the mysterious and unfathomable nature of the cat. It is nigh on impossible to tell what a cat is thinking at any one point – do they want to go through the door or not – what exactly is wrong with the food on their plate – why on earth are they wailing at 3 in the morning when everyone else is asleep: and human minions aspire to this level of mysteriousness.

The minions have watched some of the catty documentaries in an effort to understand those 'who must be obeyed' and find that neither Dinozzo nor I conform to the research that these 'cat experts' have completed. They say that cats do not like sharing space and if 2 unrelated

---

[2] Dictionary.com

cats live in a house they will keep themselves apart, yet Dinozzo and I are often to be found sharing the minions' bed, no quarrelling, no arguing, just a lot of snoozing. They say it is the top cat that comes for attention and the cats at the lower orders have to stay away, yet it is I who sits on Minion 1's lap whenever it is available day or night, and Dinozzo who has a more selective approach to minion attention. The researchers say that cats have evolved to be 'more like dogs' so that they can better train their minions to do their will. I agree that I understand when Minion 1 starts to count then I have until she reaches 5 to decide whether or not I should walk through the door that is currently being held open for me, but I will not under any circumstances fetch a stick for anyone.

Why is the aloofness of a cat prized? I believe it is for this reason. Human minions like to be dominated. They need to know where their place is in the social order, and they feel most comfortable when such boundaries are in place. This is best achieved by keeping the minions guessing as to what you are actually thinking at any one time. Are you pleased or annoyed, will you purr or scratch, is that a fur ball or are you about to vomit? In this manner it is possible to keep your minions kowtowing to your every whim.

The truth of the matter is that we cats are not really inscrutable; it is not that we are mysterious or unfathomable; it is not that our thoughts are difficult to understand. It is mostly that at any one point in time we haven't actually decided ourselves what we think or feel about anything. Do we want to walk through the door – who knows? I certainly haven't made my mind up about that yet, and why should I tell you?

Cats vs. Dogs

The age-old dilemma of which animal is better – the cat or the dog – is one that seems to have plagued humankind for centuries. The ancient Egyptians of course were renowned for worshipping the cat as gods, and had large statues dedicated to them. Other forms of cat worship have been practiced and in my opinion this is a long forgotten tradition that needs to be re-instated.

In the meantime dogs have manipulated their simple and oafish ways into the hearts of minions. Dogs give the impression that it is the minion who is in command, and that they are subservient to the minions. But, let's look at the facts. Who has to earn the money to buy the food to put in the bowl and pick up the poop, and who gets to eat tasty treats and sleep on the bed? In reality, dogs too see their minions as just that – minions: they're just better at hiding it.

There is a TV show on at the moment which pits the different skills of cats against dogs in an effort to demonstrate which of the animals is superior to the other. It's an interesting debate, and it is true that in some areas, such as 'smell' dogs are better endowed than cats. They certainly are much smellier anyway. However, the show misses the point. Each animal contributes toward the household in different ways because that is the way that we have learned to live over the years. The dogs may run around on the farm herding sheep to help the farmer and in so doing run for 30 miles a day, but it is the cats using their short bursts of running energy that catch the mice and rats which protects the animal feed or crops that the farmers bring in. Both animals in this regard are superior to each other in the field in which they work. I do grant you that a Jack Russell can also do a fair amount of damage to a room of rodent pests as well, but I'm sure a large cat such as a lion could partake in sheep herding if they put their minds to it.

I take issue with the research which suggested that dogs were more intelligent than cats because they could distinguish more dots from fewer dots on 2 screens. What sort of an intelligence test is that I ask you? How to get a minion to open a door for you when you are more than capable of making it through the cat-flap on your own – that is a real test of intelligence. How to communicate to your minion to turn over so that you can sleep on their stomach rather than anywhere else on the bed: that takes intelligence. Who needs to know that 3 is more than 1 when you're a solitary hunter and you can identify your kittens by individual smell?

You will be surprised to know that I am not saying that cats are better than dogs. However, in the time that I have shared a house with a dog there have always been a number of cats and the 1 dog and the dog has always been at the bottom of the social hierarchy in this household. I leave you to make your own conclusions.

Cattitude

Cattitude is the attitude that only cats can produce toward their minions and those inferior to themselves. It is the flattening of the ears and the turn of the head which says 'whatever' to whomever has just remonstrated with them. It is the gait and swing of the hips which states 'I meant to do that' when the cat has just fallen from a chair or got its claw caught in something and needed assistance with extraction. It is the complete sense of 'being right and beyond reproach or ridicule' that cats have at all times.

I personally am not the greatest exponent of cattitude, I am too self-effacing, modest, co-operative, vocal and old to demonstrate cattitude at its best. Empress Ziva, the diva, was the best in this area; she possessed cattitude with a capital CAT. Without any compunction, she would sleep in the dog's crate and when told to quit the property, as it was the dog's bedtime, would bite the dog before walking out head held high, wafting her tail and flattening her ears whilst Minion 1 told her off, as if to say, 'Do I look bothered?'. She could also on occasion be spotted falling off a fence or other location whereupon she would look around, check to see who was watching and make that same jaunty walk as she headed back into the house with an air of 'nothing to see here'.

It was this cattitude which meant that the minions would catch her batting me or Dinozzo or even themselves as they walked past on occasions. It was cattitude that meant, on the rare moments that I sought to overpower her for the seat nearest to the fire, she would soundly thrash me. As I returned to the assault 5 minutes later I would receive another sound thrashing, and this cycle of attempted coup and thrashing would repeat until one of the minions would come over and remove me from the hearthrug. This same cattitude allowed the dog to sit with her in front of the fire because Abi was so low down the pecking order she wasn't even worth noticing.

Dinozzo, as the new top cat, has tried to demonstrate instances of 'cattitude'. He has some elements of this approach, his wanton attitude to batting Minion 1 for example when she has given him some fuss and attention and he wants it to continue; his gentle batting of me when I come too close and he is on Minion 2's knee. However, he doesn't have the ruthless streak that is necessary for the proper exercise of true cattitude. I'm sure he believes he's superior to everyone else; he just can't always be bothered to let everyone else know. Perhaps as he matures and his kittenish moments dwindle his true catty cattitude will appear.

As for me I am far too wise, considerate, and understanding of the other species with whom I co-exist and over whom I have dominion to be a true aficionado of cattitude. I admire it in others; I appreciate its value as something which keeps right relationships within a household. I just think it takes too much effort to pull off well, and truth be told I'm just too old and tired and I really can't be bothered. Cattitude…a younger cats' game.

Fireworks

The season for Guy Fawkes, New Year and Chinese New Year has been and gone, and Diwali has passed and with it too has the sound of hissing, and crackling and small explosions that accompany the fireworks that are set off over this period. I am a fairly laid-back character and somewhat deaf to boot, and so am not too perturbed by these events. In addition my minions tend to lock the cat flap so that I cannot be outside to watch these fiery creations, but instead I snooze inside while the bangs and whizzes continue unabated outside.

I believe the minions used to quite like fireworks but since the acquisition of Abi they have taken a very different viewpoint of it. Abi is a gentle soul and does not understand the whooshes and the whizzes and finds them distressing. On a bad day she will sit on her minion's lap panting in distress and on occasions has had to be sedated with Valium.

I know that Abi is not the only dog that suffers in this way from fireworks, and I also know some cats are quite frightened by them as well. In addition my minion is informed by her mother that the foxes and badgers that she feeds nightly do not visit when there are fireworks about, which must mean that they go hungry as they stay holed up in their dens at night. Minion 1 also spent time living in Afghanistan where she regularly heard gun-fire and explosions and to her the sound of fireworks is reminiscent of that noise. As a result she does not like fireworks and no longer watches them.

I'm not against fireworks per se: everyone likes to have some fun, and they are enjoyable to watch. However, I am intrigued as to how one night of fireworks can last two weeks, with explosions to be heard regularly throughout the fortnightly period. I appreciate that not everyone can celebrate on the same night but surely there has to be some moderation in this. Harmony is achieved when we all have our basic needs met and we all have a basic need for fun and entertainment. Surely we all have a basic need for safety and security as well and this can be disturbed by constant fireworks.

I know that Abi is a bit of a wimp at times, but she is what she is. Can we spare a thought for her and the other animals that suffer at fireworks time and perhaps limit them to the weekends only?

I prefer the other types of fireworks, the ones that go off when Abi and Dinozzo are chasing a squirrel in the garden. I can watch these from the comfort of the back lawn while animals fly everywhere and the squirrels then taunt them by chattering at them just out of reach. Those are good fireworks. I would suggest we have more of those instead.

Chickens – Part One

Last week the minions rescued some battery hens. They were acquired through the British Hen Wildlife Trust and were carried home 2 to a cat crate – my cat crate I might add and without my permission. Anyway, they arrived home and were due to go out in the carefully erected fox, dog, and cat-proof enclosure that very afternoon. However, these particular four ladies (Jenny, Duckie, Furnell and Proby) were all bald, and with the temperatures as low as they are at the moment could not go outside as they would die of hypothermia apparently: which suggests to me that they need to change to wearing fur instead of feathers, but I suppose they can only work with what they've been given.

The minions did take them out one afternoon for a few hours when it was relatively warm, but as the 4 girls crowded around their feeder they were caught by the chill breeze and all of them started to shiver immediately. In the meantime Abi stood outside the fence staring intently at the new arrivals clearly with the desire to see if any of their remaining feathers could be ruffled in a short chase around their new enclosure. Unfortunately she soon discovered that the fence was in fact electrified and although she had been told not to touch it managed to give herself a short sharp shock on 2 separate occasions despite the fact she'd been nowhere near a juvenile detention centre. Soft wet quivering nose aside Abi soon recovered and the chickens were once again gathered up and brought inside where they are now living in the basement.

I personally have not seen their temporary living quarters. I am told that even though it is only 6 metres square it is still 6 times the amount of space that they had in their cages in the battery farm, and that their new feathers are slowly beginning to grow through. The basement contains the boiler, the water tank and a radiator so is quite warm even when it is very cold outside. I hear the birds making particularly strange noises, and understand that the minions put them to bed at night and let them out in the morning. From the smell emanating under the doorway I can tell these chickens are not litter trained. Abi too is quite keen to see them at close quarters when not separated from them by an electric fence, but as yet has only been able to stand in the kitchen with her head through the cat-flap whining whilst the minions are dealing with the 'chooks' in the basement.

The downside of the hens is that even in their poor bedraggled state they are still producing eggs and the minions have collected their first dozen eggs in less than a week. This is really most unacceptable in my opinion. How on earth am I to maintain my status as a non-contributory member of the household, when these battered birds are producing food for consumption every day? If the bees start producing honey I will be in real trouble. My modelling days are over and regardless of all my charm I am too old and un-athletic to get the job of the ginger tom in the Go-Cat adverts. I shall have to continue advising and assisting the minions in their day to day existence to ensure that my presence in the household is truly appreciated.

I look forward to the days when the hens will be feathered again, and will be able to wander around their run, and on gardening days assist minion 1 in turning over the soil in the borders. They should be easier to stalk on those days, and although they may be bigger than me I would fancy my chances in paw-to-wing combat with any one of them. I'll keep you posted.

Lego

Every cat, no matter how young or old, needs some stimulation to keep their brains sharply honed. I understand it is much the same for the minions, though to be truthful I see little evidence of brains being honed to a point of sharpness, but I digress. Minion 2 employs the use of little plastic bricks, built into a variety of shapes and sizes for his brain stimulation. I'm not sure how it works, but he keeps various models in a particular room which is termed 'the Lego room'.

When Empress Ziva was alive this was the temple in which Minion 2 was allowed to worship her. As soon as he entered the room Ziva would run from wherever she was laying and come into the room and demand the attention that she so rightly deserved as top animal in the house. Very often she would need so much adoration that she would actually stop Minion 2 from working with any of the plastic bricks in question. Since Ziva's untimely demise Dinozzo has taken over this room as his spot for catty adoration by the minions. Once adoration and worship has stopped, then Dinozzo likes to sit in the room and interact with the bricks and on these occasions, I like to join in the melee. Dinozzo isn't always willing for me to enter the room, but generally keeps his reproofs to a gentle batting as I walk past, unlike Ziva who would insist

I leave the room, follow me out and give me a sound beating.

The reason for staying in the room is that these little plastic bricks are quite stimulating for us as well. Obviously our paws don't function so that we can make things with them, but all of the structures that exist can be used for head rubbing in general, scratching in particular, and for periodic batting. The crane for example can often be batted so that it falls over, and individual Lego pieces on the floor are fun to scoop up and flick across the room. Minion 2 also has a Lego train which is fun to slowly follow around the room as it disappears under the bridge and in the tunnel.

Periodically Minion 2 will peer at us over his glasses and say, 'is that helping?' to which the answer is obviously 'not in his opinion'; however I believe he is missing an opportunity to share in the creative processes with us. Surely the barn would look better flattened, the wind turbine on its side to artistically represent the impact of climate change on the rural economy. A derailed train gives far more scope for Lego activity with paramedics, and firemen and police officers as well as legions of injured mini-figures. Why stick to the narrow parameters of what looks good, when you have a catty imagination to play with? Surely my knocking things over as I walk through the tableaux is indicative of the decline of a decadent consumerist society, and should in fact be on display in the Tate Modern along with anything Tracey Enim has to offer?

Of course after such activities we are usually encouraged to leave the room so that Minion 2 can continue with his Lego building in peace. Whereupon, after such bouts of creative excitement, I need to go and have a little lie down. Being the next Pablo Picatsso is very hard work you understand.

What's in a Name?

As I'm sure you are aware Chaircat McGee is the honorary title given to me for the purposes of writing this blog. We had considered calling me Chaircat Miaow, but following the cyberattacks on Sony and other companies originating out of China we decided it would be politic to give me a less potentially inflammatory title. When Minion 1 and 2 originally collected me from the RSPCA my name was Shaun. There is of course nothing wrong with the name Shaun, Minion 1 having the female derivative of that name, and Minion 2 having the anglicised version of that name, but this did not fit in with the NCIS motif of nomenclature that the minions had in mind and so my name was changed. I'd like to say to protect the innocent, but there are no innocent parties here.

If you are a follower of the hit US show NCIS you may have already noticed that the names of us three cats McGee, Ziva and Dinozzo, the dog Abi, and the (now) 6 chickens Jenny, Furnell, Proby, Duckie, Bishop and Delilah all have links to that particular show. This is slightly problematic where the show tends to feature strong male leads and the minions have surrounded themselves with female animals and birds, but nonetheless, with a little changing of gender stereotypes the names Duckie and Furnell have been brought into a new feminine light. Minion 1 tells me though when I am 'gone' they will replace me with 3 kittens from the RSPCA and call them Leroy, Jethro and Gibbs. As I have no intention of 'going' anywhere I do not know when they think that is likely to happen.

However, despite my assigned name the minions tend to call me a variety of things. McGee McGoo, oh with your eyes so blue…. Magicals, Grumpelstiltskin, the Miaow miaow monster, the snot monster, and on occasion 'the ginger furbag'. Minion 1 in particular refers to me as 'my big fella'. All of these names are of course given with the due respect and deference that I am entitled to as Deputy top cat, and most wise and sagacious member of the household, I am sure. No-one of course knows my real name. I don't mean the name that I had before I was rescued by the RSPCA, but the name that my mother gave me when I was but a little kitten. It is a name which implies great wisdom and strength, and one worthy of utmost respect, something like 'warrior-king cat', but not that because that would be giving it away.

I of course bear no resemblance to my NCIS namesake. He is neither ginger, a follower of Confucius or as craggily handsome as me. I am not a computer geek and merely employ the laptop as a means of writing my blog and downloading my favourite films such as Garfield. I do get hit on the back of the head a lot by Dinozzo and that may be where we have much in common. The television McGee is also a writer, a talent that I possess and perhaps I too will one day publish under a 'nom-de-plume'. Keep an eye out for 'the quotations of Chaircat McGee' and 'The Little Red Book of Chaircat McGee' – and 'some more of my miaows'. Hopefully I,

like a good episode of NCIS will be able to keep you
entertained for many years to come.

Chickens - Part Two

Since my first post regarding the chickens, a number of things have happened. Firstly, the minions decided to get two more chickens (Bishop and Delilah) to add to the four they already had (Jenny, Duckie, Furnell and Proby), and all six chickens were eventually placed outside in the run where they have now bonded and formed a large chicken-like mass. At first I thought these birds were harmless creatures, indeed I thought I could best any of them in combat. However, I have now had the chance to study them from afar, that is the living room patio door, and I can see that these birds are in fact exceptionally dangerous. They move around as a swarm, pecking and scratching at everything they see. When they are allowed out of their run into the garden nothing is safe from them as they roam around in search of easy pickings. Initially I thought that I would only have to contend with their wings in combat, but I hadn't realised the size of their beaks or talons at the time. These are not creatures that you want to engage in mortal combat.

I question the intelligence of my minions. Do they not know that these birds are descended from velociraptors? It is possible that we will all be murdered in our beds. I have to be extra vigilant at night, wandering around the house, miaowing at the slightest noise in case it is they who have broken in to kill us and eat us while we sleep. I know they are locked inside a chicken coop with an electric fence on, but still I think the minions are taking unprecedented risks with our lives. In protest I have refused to go out into the garden since their arrival. I stand at the back door and stare at them intently seeking to overpower them with my superior catty brain, but their squawking and head movements are hypnotic and I feel myself falling under their spell. The only way to stay safe is to flee into the house.

Minion 1 is using the 'ham bribery' ploy to get me to go into the garden. This is the technique we used when Empress Ziva was scared by a large cat and refused to go outside for a number of weeks. Judicious use of ham as a positive reward for entering the garden, plus the spreading of wet cat litter around the borders, and sending the dog out as an advance cat clearing tool all helped her to regain her confidence to go outside again. At the moment, the 'ham technique' has enabled me to find the strength and courage to face my feathered demons and to step out onto the patio. However, I was slightly disconcerted when the chickens saw Minion 1 proffering Dinozzo and myself some ham earlier today and they legged it over to the back door as quickly as their scaly little legs would carry them. It was like something out of Jurassic Park, and I was just able to muster enough courage to stay seated in the doorway whilst Minion 1 fed me copious amounts of ham. As a technique it may yet be successful, in the meantime I get to eat a lot of nice food whilst I decide whether it is or not.

I have told the minions that I will not tolerate any further poultry or fowl additions to our household. The duck plans have to go on hold, and we are to have clearly defined times of access to the back garden when the chickens will be under lock and key. I know they will do my will…Chaircat McGee has miaowed.

Cloggers

Blogging as a form of expression has grown in past years and it now appears that almost anyone and everyone has some form of blog. These have expanded into video blogging or vlogging – as I'm given to understand they are called – and I recently completed a brief search on the internet of all the cat bloggers or cloggers that are currently active online.

My first search sent me to the website which highlighted the top 20 cat blogs! I immediately searched them to examine the erudite wit and profound insights into the feline condition that were to be offered. I was shocked, nay, appalled to see the first 'clog' which was a young Devon rex cat who regularly 'modelled' cute little kitty outfits for the camera and had her own Facebook account. What has become of the state of felinehood I thought, where are the wise words, where are the sagacious comments, where are the instructions by which humankind can lead a happy and harmonious life? Instead what I see was a parody of cat hood parading around in a tutu and other 'charming' outfits.

Reeling from disbelief I carried on searching for cloggers with whom I had fellow feeling. I found plenty of blogs that were not written by cats, but by people who gave insights into cat life, and the needs of cats. This was at least something I could see as beneficial, and although not actually 'cloggers' they were useful blogs written about cats that might be helpful for some other cat whose minions weren't really sure what to do with the mystical creature that had come to live amongst them.

I did find a few other proper cloggers but I felt that they were hiding their true catty nature, and certainly none of them expressed with anywhere near enough confidence the elements that would bring about peace and harmony to the universe. Perhaps this is just 'yin and yang'. They are the 'Yin' to my 'Yang' where they offer darkness (and I can assure you a cat dressing up in a tutu is pretty dark indeed) I offer light and goodness to those who follow me. I guess we offer a complete view of feline holistic living, but personally I think being a cat has enough problems without promoting kitty porn on the internet.

Probably the best clogs are the ones written by the Cats Protection League who are of course concerned about the welfare of felines all over the UK, and Tom Cox[3] has also written a number of books, vlogs, and clogs which are worth taking a peek at. At least they leave the cat with some dignity and honour and at no point have I seen his little black cat wearing a tutu.

I enjoy clogging immensely; I feel it allows me to express myself meaningfully to an appreciative audience and to enable non-cat owners to benefit from my years of wisdom. However my minions feel that I do plenty of clogging as it is…clogging up the airwaves with a wall of miaows at all hours of the night… clogging up the hallway carpet with little clumps of cat fur... clogging up the hoover with aforementioned lumps of cat fur… clogging

---

[3] Tom-Cox.com

up tissues with special projectile cat snot. I fear they are less appreciative of all my clogging efforts… plebs!

Holidays

Periodically the two minions flee from their responsibilities to care for Dinozzo and I, and they disappear. This action, in my opinion, is a complete desertion of duties on their part. They give us little warning, though the appearance of the 'suitcase' is a subtle hint and then take off in the car with the dog and are gone for who knows how long. Admittedly it is sometimes only for one night, but Dinozzo and I never know.

Minion 1 usually comes to tell us they are going, and tries to reassure us with kind words that they will return and we will be looked after in their absence. While they are gone Minion X appears. I have not bothered to give them an assigned number as they occasionally change and I don't want to make the effort to learn to count. Needless to say, Minion X appears, we are fed, I let them give me some fuss and attention to make them feel better, I usually sneeze on them, and then they leave.

When the minions last abandoned us the chickens were placed back in the basement so that it was easier for Minion X to look after them. This meant that the garden was pterodactyl free for the duration and I once again got to go outside to do my ablutions in peace. The sun even came out while they were gone which meant that I could rest my weary bones in the sun without fear of harm or molestation, and I took advantage of this. Warily I would pass the sounds of clucking coming from the other side of the basement and quickly make my escape through the cat-flap and into the great outdoors.

The major downside of the minions' departure is that there is no-one to keep Dinozzo in check. It is true that he does keep a low-key topcatness about him, but he is still relatively young and so has his kittenish moments when he wants to play tag. As I have said I don't mind the occasional game of 'pounce' with the dog, she knows better than to actually touch me and gives me a wide berth as she runs around the garden, but Dinozzo has no such respect for his elders. I am indeed an elderly cat with sagging bones and stiff joints and being rugby tackled or chased up the stairs as he tries to remove my one remaining good back leg is not proper Confucian behaviour by any stretch of the catty imagination. As his deputy I cannot rebuke him, or point out the error of his ways, and usually leave these to the minions who will come to my defence and tell him off. Without them about I am at the mercy of his playful whims.

There are many ways to wreak revenge on the minions for their absences. The favourite is a deposit of vomit somewhere for them to find on their return. However, last week I perfected the act of revenge by laying outside on the back lawn very still in the sunshine. As I heard the car approach I sucked in my stomach so that I looked very flat and waited for the minions to spot me. Minion 1's 'oh no!' was audible from the church next door as she gazed upon my crumpled body and thought that I had passed onto a higher plane. Dinozzo ran past me with no apparent concerns for my wellbeing in his desire to welcome them home, and once shaken with Minion 1's hand I had to demonstrate that I was in fact, still very much alive.

I am glad that we are back together. I miss the portable lap by day and my human hot water bottles by night. I miss waking them up in the small hours just so that they will give me a stroke, and I really miss sneezing on them when they are in bed. Simple things, but these are the things which make relationships so special. I hope they appreciate all the effort I put in.

Sitting Comfortably?

Sitting and sleeping are almost full time occupations for your average cat. On a good day, we will spend around 18 – 20 hours asleep, dreaming big dreams, and snoring loud snores. Achieving this takes some considerable time and effort though. If one is to spend such a length of time in an unconscious manner then it is necessary to ensure that one is fully comfortable before this can happen. This, of course, is made far more complicated when a minion and their lap is involved.

Generally I find that I need to seek the bounciest part of my minion's lap: this is usually either the bowel or the bladder or the upper stomach or the spleen, depending upon time of day. On these occasions I try to position myself so that all four paws are on the particular body part and then knead it gently, slowly lowering myself upon the desired location. If my minion shifts position I then have to relocate myself slowly, which usually involves circling round on the area for a few turns before trying to resettle. I will then once again attempt to lower myself into the desired location. Should none of the relevant body parts be particularly full, I then need to place a paw on each area so that I can get maximum 'bounce' from my support.

I have discovered that however, there is a significant mathematical relationship between myself and my minions comfort at these times. My comfort levels are inversely proportional to the comfort levels of my minion. As I become more comfortable bouncing around on her lap, she becomes less so. This is of little interest to me generally, she is above all here to serve, but if she becomes too uncomfortable that usually precipitates a move to the toilet, or being placed upon the settee instead, whereupon I then have to begin finding my comfortable spot all over again. I can assure you that spending so much time trying to get comfortable can be very wearing indeed for a cat of my growing maturity and years. So, the key is to find that acceptable balance whereby I am comfortable enough, and my minion is bearably uncomfortable, so that she doesn't feel the need to alter the status quo.

That is how class struggle works: those in control have to be just comfortable enough, and those under their control have to be bearably uncomfortable so that they don't alter the way you want life to be. If the balance tips too much in favour of the superiors – such as myself – then the minions start revolting, and I can tell you my minions can be quite revolting at times. It's a stoic lesson in learning not to be too self-centred and to make sure that harmony reigns in the household.

I do eventually have to get moved, partly because my minions refuse to sit still for the 8 hour bursts of sleeping that I need to maintain my craggy good looks. However, I like to get my own back by waiting until they are dropping off at night and then parading into the bedroom miaowing loudly until I am scooped up and placed on the bed, where I can start 'sitting comfortably' again on my minion's body while she tries to sleep. Remembering the rule always – comfortable enough v. bearably uncomfortable is the way to maintain the status quo.

Training Cats

Much is made of the ability to teach dogs to do things such as 'sit', 'wait', or 'come', though if the noises I can hear gently drifting over from the park behind us are anything to go by, the latter command is not one which is easily learned. Cats of course are really above such things, we already know an awful lot, and there is little that we need to learn for our own benefits, but occasionally a little assistance is needed for us to learn to do something which will of course be a long-term benefit to us in the future.

I do not, of course, refer to learning to use an indoor toilet. I am more than aware that it is possible; I have even seen a video of some poor cat attempting to cover up its 'scat' with copious amounts of paper having done the requested deed in the toilet. I though, believe it is beneath the dignity of a cat to do such an activity and would rather 'poop' in the back garden or in the cat litter tray nearest the radiator when it's a cold and wet day/night outside. What I refer to is the occasional use of ham by one or both minions to 'encourage' us to do the things that make life easier for us.

When Dinozzo first joined our harmonious household, he did not know how to use a cat flap, and following a difficult altercation with the flap one day in which he got his paw stuck he was keen not to use the kitty portal again. In an effort to encourage him the minions waited until he wanted to come back in through the back door and then waved ham at him from the other side. The poor little mite struggled for some time desperately stabbing the area around the cat flap with his paws until he struck gold and managed to push the flap open. Unlike Empress Ziva or myself, who were quite able to head butt our way in through the door, sometimes at speed, little Dinozzo was anxious not to touch the cat flap if at all possible and it was only the added motivation of some ham which gave him the courage to push his way through. Once he had got the hang of this the minions would throw some ham through the cat flap and then watch him jump through afterwards. As he became more confident with the flap if he let himself in or out without assistance he was immediately rewarded with some ham, which meant that he jumped in and out of the cat flap on a number of occasions when he didn't particularly want to go outside.

Ziva found the use of ham helpful in overcoming her scare by a large catty garden intruder, along with some other help from the minions, and I too have found my feet and my courage to return to the back garden once again with some prompting from a piece of ham waved at me from 20metres. I have even managed to find my own way out into the garden on occasion, and am rewarded with some ham once I have made my way back in.

Of course, I would have eventually managed to find my way back into the garden without the aid of ham, but this little technique makes the minions think they know what they are doing, and in the meantime, I get to eat as many treats as a cat can eat. I think that counts as a win-win scenario. Peace and harmony reign once more in this catty household.

Paparazzi

I understand that in the circles of the rich and famous the presence of the paparazzi is an unavoidable burden which at best can be tolerated and at worst brings the worst out in those that are being photographed. Since I have begun my 'clogs' on a regular basis, and have developed my Facebook page, it would appear that I am too a victim of these creatures. However, I am perplexed, if not a little discombobulated, to see that my photographic hunters are mostly Minion 1 and Minion 2. There are no high speed chases as I am pursued on the back of a motorbike, or photographed from 500m away with a super zoom lens. No, I am picked off where I am at my most vulnerable and weak…asleep on the settee.

I know that with fame comes the need to engage with a growing fan base, and that photos of me looking 'cute' are a way to do this. Unfortunately, I am not a cat that does cute particularly well. I do disgruntled quite well, sleepy with a reasonable level of skill, and snotty with little or no thought on the matter. It is true that when curled up asleep on the settee with my front paws quivering as I run in my sleep and have my tongue sticking out at the same time I have a certain cute 'je ne sais quoi', but for the life of me I don't know what, and I don't know why humans like it so much.

At the moment, the minions are in search of a suitable joint 'headshot' of Minion 1 and me together for the Production Department at the publishers for publicity purposes. I am not entirely sure why minion 1 has to appear in the picture at all and so I refuse to co-operate with them as she seeks to ride along on the coat-tails of my success. Plans to take a photo are easily subverted, and generally just involve me refusing to look at the camera, or sneezing on Minion 1 when she is trying to get an endearing photo of the pair of us looking at each other. I refuse to prostitute myself in this manner: my image is not up for sale to the highest bidder. I am a cat of distinction, wisdom and merit. I do not do photo opportunities and if I had a fully functioning pair of back legs I'd be able to keep out of the way – and of course if I didn't need to sleep for 20 hours a day in a location where they can easily find me. Earlier today I had to resort to hiding in one of the many woodpiles out the back. Admittedly this was as much to avoid the chickens as to avoid having my photo taken, but these are the depths to which I must stoop to evade harassment in my own back garden. Oh, how I can relate to the Duchess of Cambridge – is there no privacy anywhere?

I suppose as my celebrity grows I must get used to these intrusions upon my snoozing time, though I am shocked and surprised that on this occasion it is the minions that cause me the most problems. I shall of course wreak my revenge with the usual mix of snot and sleep deprivation. I am now, very well practiced at this particular dark art.

Chickens – The Saga Continues

The minions have persisted in keeping those feathered harpies out in the back garden. They remain lethal and poised to strike at any moment. The other day Delilah, the chicken at the bottom of the pecking order, managed to see off Dinozzo and Abi at the same time. Admittedly Dinozzo was only running over to see the minions and when Delilah took exception to his close presence to her went into strike mode. Abi, seeing the confrontation, ran over as peace maker and was immediately repelled as the chicken hunched her shoulders and fixed her beady little eye on Abi's jugular vein. This creature is the least of the velociraptors. Imagine what the top chicken is like – or even worse, if they were to act as a swarm. These creatures have no concept of respectful right relationships outside of their own flock, and seek to be at the top of every pecking order. None of them display the appropriate deference or respect to me due to my age and superior rank in life.

For this reason, I continue nightly to prowl around the bed at 2 hourly intervals to ensure that everyone is alert and awake in case of attack. I feel able to sleep during the day for 8 hours at a stretch myself because the minions are awake and so are able to protect themselves if the need arises, but at night they are of course vulnerable and it is my role to ensure their safety. Minion 1 has taken to getting up as soon as I make a noise and putting me on the bed to stroke me in an effort to placate me, and because I know that she is now awake and alert to any potential chickeny threats I feel able to fall asleep again too, but only for a couple of hours.

It has been suggested that I am showing early signs of dementia in cats, but I know better. Whilst Dinozzo and Abi sleep on in dereliction of their duties, I alone am responsible for the safety and security of the house and to ensure that the chickens don't slit our throats and eat our gizzards while we sleep.

However, having spent time in Zen meditation, I have discovered my 'inner' tiger and am now able to spend time in the back garden whilst the chickens are out and about. This is mostly prompted by the presence of sunshine and a need to soak my old bones in its warmth, and I at no point fall asleep out there whilst they are out scratting at the soil. But, I am now able to undertake the cat essentials outside, and to enjoy the breeze and feel the sun on my face.

I know that suffering is part of life and so have steeled myself to face this daily assault on my peace and security. I recite my catty mantras - 'I am tiger: hear me roar', which can be heard from some distance away according to the minions, and centre myself in a peaceful frame of mind. I also keep one eye on the nearest entrance to the house and ensure that I sit in a location where nothing can sneak up behind me. I may not be a Zen master, but neither am I complete fool.

Cat Breath

Being a mature cat of advancing years and struggling with living with Feline Leukaemia Virus I occasionally suffer with a snot/fur ball combo which causes me to hack significantly in quite a melodramatic way until I can shift the offending obstruction from my windpipe. Minion 1 is usually pretty good in adding the assistance of a few taps between the shoulder blades to help, but Minion 2 always comments 'catty breath!' afterwards. I find such observations insulting and offensive. Surely if he too had to summon strength from the very bowels of his being to remove a large globule of fur and snot then he too might find that the aroma of his stomach contents is then diffused throughout the area.

In my defence cats do at least only eat things that constitute food. I appreciate this is a wide definition of the word food and can include small furry rodents, reptiles, amphibians and/or fish. Admittedly I have consumed none of these things. Minion 1 and Minion 2 did find me gnawing on a concussed squirrel one day, but the state of its concussedness was nothing to do with me, being of poorly knee and gnarly toothed. Thus, I am generally confined to tinned cat food, the occasional egg yolk and the juice from the tuna can, despite my repeated protestations that some freshly cooked fish, beef or chicken might suffice. Though latterly I have begun to rethink the desire to eat chicken as I cannot shake the image of those semi-bald harpees bearing down on me in the garden and I now find the idea of chicken entirely repugnant. In any event, I know that it is possible for people to eat squirrels, if not rats and mice or lizards and so most of what I eat would be considered edible by minions' standards. Dogs on the other hand are thoroughly disgusting creatures who will eat anything that vaguely smells of food. Our own dear Abi, who I have deemed to treat with the cordiality and respect that a member of the household deserves from me, is in fact a thoroughly mucky pup. I know that I am to be adored and venerated, but even I would suggest that eating my poop goes beyond the pale. Abi on the other hand quite enjoys nibbling on my faecal deposits if she can get her teeth on them, much to the annoyance of the minions. In addition she will also eat sheep, chicken and horse poo if she can get to it before the minions spot her.

When such grossness is taken into consideration how can Minion 2 chastise me for having catty breath I ask? Surely, even he must know that in the Dog Vs Cat debate that wages on, it is dogs that win the war of halitosis. The contents of their stomachs can only be guessed at, and even if they do insist on feeding Abi mint flavoured dentastix one doggy belch will undermine its impact. I remain aggrieved, hurt and a little affronted, and to prove my point I shall go and sneeze on him with maybe a side order of catty breath.

Cupboards

Every cat has a deep desire to explore, to seek new worlds, to boldly go where no cat has gone before. It is hard-wired within their psyche, an unyielding force that cannot be countered and one that drives them on ever forwards, ever onwards, in the search for adventure and excitement. For most domestic cats this all-consuming need is met through their insistence on entering every single cupboard whose door is left open, examining the contents in detail and then solidly refusing to come out.

I have perfected this art and am able to tell at quite a distance when a cupboard door that is usually left closed has been opened. Even in my slightly deaf and rather doddery state I can tell at 100 paces when a hitherto hidden spot has become available. My favourite dark places are of course in the airing cupboard, but any available place with a lockable door and a shelf will do: the kitchen, the study, the bedroom, or the garage. I am ready and willing to fling myself into the perilous adventure of entering the deep and dark spaces that lead to the parallel universe of kitty adventure. Of course, within this parallel universe I seek a Narnian-Utopia, whereby all creatures speak cat and I am heralded as the long-awaited 'saviour' that will lead my newly found comrades into a time of peace and security with me as their head. All that is necessary for this to happen is for me to find the relevant cupboard that leads there.

For some reason the minions are much less keen on this catty activity and I find myself unceremoniously plucked from whatever dark and exciting new play space I have discovered. I haven't even had time to examine the crevices for a potential new world to explore when I am asked, nay – ordered, to remove myself from my new adventure playground. Should I be slow in responding to their unnecessary demands then I am forcibly removed. Occasionally, they will just close the door on me, count to ten, and then open the door again so that I can get out. If I choose to settle in quiet repose instead, they are unhappy. I find that there is literally no pleasing them. Fortunately, that isn't a goal that I aim to achieve.

I believe minions could benefit from developing that cat-like ability to examine even the mundane with the potential for excitement and adventure. In this way a pen lid is suddenly transported into a play-thing; a cupboard becomes an adventure play-ground; and a chicken becomes a thing of mortal terror. In this way minions will develop that excellent sense of curiosity that is much admired in cat-kind. They will find themselves exploring new avenues of possibility, and perhaps they too will acquire the concomitant 9 lives necessary to go with this risky lifestyle.

In the meantime, I shall continue on my valiant quest as I seek out new civilisations, I will still be happy if I find a quiet, warm place to have my daily 44 winks.

Cat Whispering

There has been an evident increase on the television, in books, and on the web of minions who claim to be able to speak with animals and sort out any 'problems' they may have. In fact Minion 1 tells me she saw a van advertising a 'female dog whisperer' the other day. I merely want to know if it was a dog whisperer who was a female – or a dog whisperer who only worked with female dogs. I am intrigued by this concept of 'whispering' as it is clear that the only creature who has the problem is the minion who cannot understand the needs of their superiors who are merely seeking to demonstrate volubly that the minion is getting it completely wrong.

My minion has also taken up whispering with me, though her attempts at whispering are basically to encourage me to stop miaowing at full volume – whatever time of day and night – and for me to produce a gentle whispering purr instead. In order to do this I must be placed in close proximity to her on the bed, settee, or on her lap when she is working at the computer, and she must gently tickle my chest until I have finished wiping my nose on the back of her hand, sneezing, hacking gently, or complaining generally about the lack of attention. I may then, all things considered, settle into a refined and delicate doze or watch her while she works and start to whisper gentle purrs.

It usually takes a few minutes for 'whispering' to come into effect because I want her to be sure exactly how much she has failed me in her cat-care duties, that I have had to wander around calling for her from the kitchen, or backyard, or had to try to get onto her lap whilst she is working at the computer in the first place. She should after all be following me around ensuring that every one of my catty whims is met: that there is an adequate pile of food in my bowl; that the chickens are not being too irritating when I am trying to snooze in the sunshine out the back; that they are not at that moment trying to break into the house and kill us all while we sleep; that Dinozzo hasn't taken my spot on the spare bed and that I am not in need of urgently required stroking and general fussing.

To be fair to her at night now she is pretty quick out the bed to pick me up when I start to miaow in the small hours. Years of training have taught her that merely ignoring me is futile as I can continue to miaow with an increasingly high-pitched squeak for some considerable time. I am a patient cat, I have learned this over the years, and I do not get bored of sharing my opinions, especially when they involve the poor level of cat-care and attention that I receive during the dark hours of the night. Equally, they have given up trying to lock me out the bedroom as I can make much more noise scratching at the bedroom door while I sing the song of my people.

The art of whispering is just to work out what your cat wants before they tell you, because if you leave it that long, I for one, will continue to tell you for a very long time. And I don't come with volume control.

Mortality

I've been feeling a bit poorly this last week or so. I am an old cat and was a little doddery on my feet so the vet was treating me for arthritis. However, I really am very tired an awful lot of the time now and don't feel like eating at all. On re-examination, the vet told my minions that she thinks I have a brain tumour. I don't know what one of these things is, but I know Minion 1 started to cry, and she and the vet started to talk about 'quality of life'.

On reflection my life has had many ups and downs. The lowest point of course was having to be rescued by the RSPCA – although my time there was pleasant enough: I had visitors every day to give me food and fuss and attention, I had some teeth removed that were giving me a lot of pain, and I bulked up to my adoption weight of 5.5 kg. It was from there that I was given the exciting opportunity to train and manage some new minions. They haven't been the easiest of minions to change, but I now have Minion 1 responding 'how high' when I ask her to jump these days, and that is very satisfying indeed.

During my 6 years with these minions I have loved and lost the beautiful Empress Ziva, who won my heart even if she did periodically beat me up, and whose death 15 months ago broke my little catty heart. I have learned to live with and in some part train Abi, another refugee who came to join us from the RSPCA and I have endeavoured to teach little Lord Dinozzo some manners and model a benign and kindly leadership approach to him. I'm less confident that he has learned that particular leadership style, but we have had comradely times together asleep on the bed and keeping each other company whilst the minions are away. Of course, the most recent adventure has been learning to live with the chickens. I can't say that I like them very much, but I am now happy to lie outside in the sun whilst they peck their way around the garden near me.

Coming from a Confucian background it is more important how I conduct my life on a day to day basis than it is to worry about the future – if I were a Buddhist I believe that I have reached the zenith of my existence as a cat and that Nirvana waits for me. Yet, I do not worry about these things. I reflect upon what has been, I focus on what is, and I leave what will happen tomorrow until tomorrow knowing that my minions love me. To truly live in the moment is a skill that all animals can teach their minions, and I have mastered this moment of living and provided a role model for teaching.

I may not be the captain of my fate or the master of my soul, but I am a cat who has enjoyed his life in its simplicity, even with all the medical issues that I have faced, and I am glad to have lived and breathed the air on a warm summers' day, and assisted in the stalking of a few squirrels.